Soft Engineering

Kate Foley

Onlywomen Press

Published in 1994 by Onlywomen Press, Ltd.
71 Great Russell Street
London WC1B 3BN

Poems by Kate Foley were first published in 1968 in *Socialist Commentary*. Since then, her poems have appeared in the *Poetry Business Anthology*, *Proof*, *Writing Women*, *Poetry Nottingham*, *Poetry Sampler 83*; readings at Lincoln Cathedral and St. Julian's Community, Sussex also included Kate's work. *"Reflections"* won second prize in the 1984 Lincoln Festival and *"My Father, counting sheep"* was first prize winner in the inaugral (1993) Margot Jane Memorial Poetry Prize judged by U.A. Fanthorpe and Marilyn Hacker.

Printed and bound in the U.K.

British Library/Cataloguing in Publication Data.
A catalogue record for this book is available from the British Library.

For Susan van El, with love

Contents

Skin sisters

Skin sisters; cheek kisses
cheek, friendly apples
bobbing together; or fierce
brass cymbals, hissing
past each other;

but nothing,
no colour of spleen
can dye me different
from where your skin
puckers on breast
or belly above the deep
heat of your wound,
or your aging freckles
mark time.

I read you in the papers,
bump you softly
in the tube; have,
gentled by a raised
eyebrow, rueful smile,
everything in common;
or nothing as you scowl,

except my soft suede,
my middle-aged skin,
squamous pavement,
cellular stepping stone
over the cracks,
down the long street
where we live, pecking past
each other at weddings
and funerals, our nerve
endings crocheted together,
kissing or killing kin.

Well, Daughter...

hoping this, a line
aimed deeper
than a wrinkle in time,
finds you –

Never mind that you
weren't a plum coloured
bawling baby, braided
with birth blood;
a child, clean
as a new pinny,
rinsed with wind
from long-legged kites
walking the common;
a teenager, collecting
worldly smuts,
angles and pain;

somewhere you are;
on the other side
of a closed door.
 Somewhere is the parcel
of birth pangs, broken nights,
wash-wrinkled hands,
measles, chicken-pox,
petulance, estrangement,
and painful love,
that belongs to me.

I am rich with its loss;
absence creates
a room for echoes.

Deep in the mirror
of my own face
you look for me.

This time I say no

This time I say no,
not up-front, but eyes
bent obstinately down
on the evening paper.

Old, dotty, good humoured
and black, her white turban
askew, her smiling lips
ploughed down by furrows,
she passes her ill-spelled
begging board before us
mandarins in our nodding row.

One day I give:
another withold;
constant as god
or the weather.

I had a bad day;
my secretary flipped;
my bowl of human kindness
is skimmed milk.

She pauses by the door;
gives a tootle-root
on a paper comb.
"Forget it folks,
see if I care."

What if I run
and kneel, and shred
my payslip before her?

We come too late
for pouring out;
cultured baccilli
keep us thin and sour;
all thrift and no spend.

Enclosures

Better than anything, I like
your ordinary occupations
to be different from mine.

At night, on either side
of this scrubbed table, set
with food I've cooked,

on plates you've washed,
you do your crossword,
I'll read my book: both

rinsed in the same clean
river of music. Daily
we pile our separate stones

on drystone walls enclosing
private places. You hedge
my bets. I mend your fences;

but going down to the bone,
love is finger printed with distance;
your grain's your own.

Seeing you, seeing me

Black lines, skeins of stems
sheafed and bunched
on a white page, make planes;
my face grows before your eyes.
I look steadily for you,
and see the black and white
abstraction of a dying fire:
black logs in the grate
chequered with ashy squares,
a white flicker, flame crumbling,
powdery soot. With thumb
and charcoal you smudge in my eyes.

What do we see, each
for the other in a black and white
landscape? Stroked charcoal
makes the space of my face
change: and the black log lies,
as evening draws on,
quietly snowing ash.

After the visitors

After the door shuts
we snap back together
into the elastic twang
of our row. I turn up
the light, see white coffee cups,
single lotuses; see your

frown etched in metal.
You see my set face,
concrete hard, ribbed,
slatted against you.
Glasses with dregs,
our eyes drained
of communication
ring in this room, now
peeled of friendly presences.

Rage is narcotic.
I forget why I hate you,
why our furniture
has killing edges,
why the colour has gone.

From the corner of my eye
I see your fisted hand
suddenly uncurl its fingers,
flutter towards me.
I remember who you are,
and why I hate you,
but my fingers, like
a time lapsed photograph
have a life of their own,
and uncurl slowly towards you.

The quail syndrome

They pair when their breast bars match,
like iron filings to the magnet,
strong lines of force,

snatch of like to like.
How the earth and tides pull
is in the mixture.

What chance has love
subverted by attraction?
The cure is hard.

Debar the nest; breast shaped
simple curve for a few
warm eggs.

Make each bird
take to its untried wings;
stake its life on air.

A question of chemistry

Do you know about axons and neurons
and chemical transmitters,
words describing the relocation of a pain
from the site of the wound
to the place of perception?

Hand to hand, across the net of skin
my blood addresses yours
in a language I can't hear,
don't speak, will never understand.

Like the strong tendrils of hair
persisting round a skull,
or roots too tough for the mattock,
you crop up.

I thought of our room as a honeycomb,
the cells orderly if organic,
a peaceable smell of beeswax in the air,
a store of nutriment growing tidily;
the occasional sting poulticed in honey.

But bees, diligent slicked-down workers
may run mad; may amplify hints
from the susurration of the hive,
become a cloud of bullets,
blind and equal
as the balance beam on which death swings.

Fruit fall

Light as bleached grass
your life moves to its end.
But listening to you tell
each story over and over
I know it has been
heavy as rich fruit cake,
half understood, as
underground rivers
can be traced
by alders near the water's rise.
Bent under the ripe weight
of my heart towards you
I listen as your fruit falls.

Mexican Day of the Dead
The Tree of Life our bones

Carnival. Harsh velvet music
on All Souls' Eve; the year's embers
blaze gold and umber on graves
heaped like market stalls.

My Grandmother is my kitchen.
She provides from her mound
pumpkins, tortillas, sugarpigs,
and the savage red breath of chili.

On my child's grave,
chocolate, bread and marigolds,
baby suns in their glass jar.

Death's logo, its vivid
black and white grin
is everywhere, a flower
tucked in its bony breeches.

Everywhere, their faces,
black and white
but framed in flowers.
Domestic as a woman
in her apron, or a man
with lathered jaws,
they look shy, bemused.

She gazes out
from her gilded frame.
Her eyes return
the steady glow
of a thousand candles.

She is my bird, her dove breast
still beats at my wrist;
her braids chain my heart;
it hangs in its blue-black net.

My little dove, your bones
the tree that shelters me,
brilliant with fruit
and pain and feathers.

Once a year we swallow
this truth. Our food
is scalding as
an Aztec's heart.
Our dead.

Making the days

It is like waving off a train,
Small and peaky, growing smaller
your face is burrowed in its chins.
Cheek skin runnelled,
old laugh lines like scars
till they flesh up firm
when you grin.

Each last bit,
a casual photo at a church fete,
an outing to the coast,-
too far to go again
your breath too raw -
is another telegraph pole
flashing past on the racketty line,
beating out the journey
with gathering tempo.

You never wanted to stop
or get off,
rather let the Christmas treat
merge with a doze in your chair.

How will you rest?
God was never responsible
for the green spears in your garden,
your profligate house plants,
or even the swallows
skimming ripe barley.

You made the world
seven times over each day
between breakfast and tea,
and peopled it,
a touch of iron
for those who strayed
beyond the picket
of your imagination.

It may be more of a day trip
than a journey, a dignity
of simply going with the wheels,
too tired to keep on
making the days.

Telling the bees

A country custom requires you to tell the bees
of a death or birth

A circular saw cutting wedges
of soft spring weather, bees
relentlessly buzz the willow,
a sharp halo of need
around silky buds.

Bees do not fold themselves up
to mourn the unassuagable loss
of summer, but crouched in
a still dark suspension
shot with light, like sun seen
through the blood of frail fingers,
they wait in certainty
of winter, until the spring clock
fires them out round the sallow.

Crossed skeins of rapid morse
led to a field patched
out of brambles, set
with small, crazy bee prefabs,
bricks holding down their lids
against a pilfering wind.
Scattered bloom of cloud
rolled across the turf,
everything turning,
lightside of leaf to dark
grass riffling, a zip undone,
bees locking onto the hive like iron filings.

I told them her name
and number of years.
God knows where they took it,
spinning planetary music
around the flight path
from hive to tree.

Rendered down

I have been in the fire.
The black flute
of my bones
is clogged with ashes.

Blow; they'll float
out, lazy as clouds,
little peace-pipe
flocks of grey.

Then the music,
clear and nourishing
as bouillon,
all my soft parts
gone to stock.

Nothing of the wild
chrysanthemum flames
shouting through
a horror of smoke.

Only this clear
music, strong food,
and my black bones.

Thrown

I bought death for our cat;
the needle, drug and vet
to kill her pain.

As I buried her, an ant
walked over one green
translucent eye.

It is relief to turn
to larger deaths. Megaliths,
part of a growing circle,

they stand so tall,
so other, so far beyond
effect of mine, that pain

is like the ant
on my cat's dead eye -
irrelevant.

I butt my head against
their granite sides;
I cannot move them.

Great stone cattle, they give
no milk, or blood; as cold
and far from tears as clouds.

It is cats and birds and empty
slippers; small lives lost
that move the stone;

they are the pebble
on which your heel turns
to bring death home.

Pillow talk

for Catherine Arthur

Shadows thick as four o'clock
in winter, scoop hollows
round your face, this Sunday noon.
The pillow sculpts your cheeks;
dew-pond still, your eyes
sink deep in darkness.

Presence and absence fight.
Your mouth wears a hint of mischief,
your forehead a frown.
Do you know now? Is it alright?
Or did the act of dying make it so?
I loved you; didn't know you;
can only read the signs.

The men come. Their arms
like clumsy wings
fold you away.

Now on the table
a half empty glass,
a spoon, a bent straw,
gathering light;
the bed is rumpled.
I see your head
has left its frown upon the pillow.

You have been growing all this while

You have been growing
all this while,
on the edge of sight.
No more visible
than you ever were,
an ironic voice
on the answer-phone.
But on that one
September day,
dripping with fat, late
catkins of light
glancing off the slats
of the white garden table,
you were there,
present and solid,
clinking golden glasses,
turning replete
towards the sun,
a boat, dipping
and trawling
on the meniscus
of our lives.

Still flushed
we all four walked
in a sunken lane
open to the river.

A small deer
lay dead and fallow
near the bridge.

Your face bleached.
I saw the piled
gold cliff of afternoon
fall on you.

When did you die,
still wound and wit
to your lover?
To me, the cooling
cheek I touched
and massive emptiness
of sheets is quick
and knobbled root
of the strange signs
and sounds I make
before I speak.

Battering baby

manacles of tenderness
ligatures of love
no blood beading
on skin soft as glove

milkywarm breathing
light as a leaf
turns into avalanche
roaring down grief

blowing apart
leaves on the wind
rub your back baby
painfully sing

soft white stalk
lolling head
bite on the jelly
baby is dead

fish in my blood
pith in my bone
hard in my heart
love like a stone

Soft engineering

Ceaselessly licking the coast
the sea is engaged in soft engineering.
She tongues up heaped, trickling spits
of shingle, as a mother cat
pridefully peaks up the wet fur of kittens.
Slick and shiny, precision smoothed
pebbles from the sea's mouth
glissade down the wave that drops them.

She is tooled up for many tasks;
not only the smoothing of freckled sands
but the saw-toothed carving of collops
from the land's edge; the spirited abrasion
of hard rock till it cuts back,
curdling the water in a mess of foam.

Relentless as mother-love
the sea builds the bone of the land
and scoops its soft, domed tilt.
But of all her multiple pregnancies,
the land will never grow up,
out of reach of that inexorable tongue.

Long grass with butterflies: Van Gogh

That grass is dangerous,
the vital fur of an animal
breathing out sun,
or an opened hand
sprawled in electric peace.
Butterflies doped with paint
stagger like bi-planes
in a blazing field of view.

Green eyes herded visions
of wild grass
through black pupils,
celebrated its circuits
in a catherine wheel brain.

The sun is stretching,
is speaking with tongues
in the grass.
You could stagger, yourself,
made half blind and deaf,
but for the path
and the shade.

Rising damp

The slow tap leaks
pregnant tears, tasting of metal,
a thin deposit, shell on shell.
Lino, blotting paper soaked,
rises to let a beetle run.
Lifted paws to labile nose,
a mouse at the window;
warmth enough
to mist a little egg shape
on the pane.

There is a mildew of the spirit
needing a cataract to clear.
Blow, gaspipe; fracture, main;
bomb flatten, roar and settle.

Ruin is palliative, but cure
is harder: to listen for
a small, clean wind.

Down in the valley

Motorway thrum. Each separate
abrasion of tyre on road
transposed by distance,
a silky, continous rustle,
the body of a great snake,
boiling from Medusa's skull,
burning through the landscape,
lifting its massive head,
the miles hissing and rippling
down its long gut.

Here, not far away, in a fold
of London's scruffy countryside,
small signs of subversion,
like laughter in church,
spike the tranced sound -
blonde streaks in the field,
brambles roughly shouldering the road,
the iron gate blistering.
Signs of ripeness, of turning,
promises of unsterile decay.

Below the hypnotic sound
an aftertaste of quiet,
like the good bitterness of medicine.

Graveyard politics

He lies beneath her,
but his name is on top
and bigger. Now
anarchic lichen
has blotted it out,
left hers crisp and clear.

Nature is on her side.
Gravitas sunk him deepest
first, left her twenty good
relict years.

As plump drips from
a self important laurel
ooze on moss,
obscure his letters,
her name, brightened
by a brisk low wind,
winks out: a modest
testament, the last small laugh.

Out of the egg

Dragon's eggs are rubbery,
will bounce, bulge elastically
at the moment of birth;
like a human caul, they allow
a small, moist, embryonic monster
to plop softly into the world,
not knock like a chick
in its china coffin.

With such a start,
what transforms the flexible bones
wearing slipery skin
vivid as new leaves, into pistons,
the mewling voice-box
into a bellows, wringing terror
from a scorched population?
What power stretches wings
so far their shadow
becomes a blight where cattle die,
five-legged lambs are born
and fish float, belly-up
in the stream?

Dragons have always had
two choices; to be a scourge
devouring maidens and cattle
(though longing for sweet grass)
or, Chinese fashion,
to coil their strength gently
round the human condition,
their breath firecracker-bright,
a brazier on frosty days.

Perhaps instead of lances
and all the whalebone
paraphernalia of chivalry,
dragons entrapped by addiction
to the flavour of terror,
need first to be distracted,
rubbed in a soft spot
rather than spitted;
introduced to a healthy diet
and left to dream of the egg.

On my birthday

I belong to a think tank,
but what I want is to think rust,
the deliquescent, encroaching
flower of iron salts,
sufficient to stop
a whole army on its tracks

Apple bud sticks

First cut your stick.
Next, pull off the leaves.
Leave only a centimetre
or so of each stalk;
then slice; a sharp,
precise, shallow incision
at thirty degrees
on each side of the bud.
Lift it out; slide it
under the prepared flap
on new stock and bind.

When you unwind
the bandage you may see
new tissue, so grown
into its host you can't find
a line, but it glows
with its own newness,
a seamless match
in a maiden tree.

Years later, thicketed
with fruit and birds,
sparsely bearded moles of lichen
fat with colour
on its evening trunk,
an apple tree still bears
somewhere in the folded
lava of its skin,
a navel scar.

Car mountain: image for Susan van El

Leaf-light, fretted sheaves
of iron, stooked in rough
bundles. Like grain-rust,
corrosion nibbles each stack
to red, brown, lichenous
blotches, umber tears. Old paint
curls like beetle cases, butterfly
sharp detritus. Crizzled glass gleams
milky or irridescent
as long buried bottle sherds.
Chrome is white as scattered bone.

Laced and bound
by fireweed, its smouldering
head and silver smoke
trembling fiercely, the whole
heap settles, trickling sound
in small parched phrases.

Time is the wheel with dented hub,
gripped by sinuous bindweed,
humming with stillness.

Emily Dickinson: dissident

A lifetime of difficult poetry.
Not for you lyricism, running blue
as dissolved snow clouds in a river.

You spoke with the bruised mouth
of a woman whose cell walls
squeezed killingly.

Yet dissonant as lightning,
truth so wounding
clears its own space: makes free.

A prayer in drought

Feed and supple
my leathery mind
with snake oil.

Brittle thoughts
dry as quartz
have sanded my skull.

Ease juice
from my dry eyes,
squeeze poppy milk

for darker dreams
rich as lake mud
old as carp.

Flood the plains
where buffalo stand
brown draped sticks.

I am not alone.
All stand under
a dry sky

praying to be joined
as H to O;
cool skin of water.

Interior

The interior plain is running
with rivers of deer,
trickling dark ribbons,
winding across a central space,
marked only by umbrella puffs of dust
and the wiry unsprung thorn;
the massif, scarred by old flash floods,
towers red in the last light;
and turning, like a snake
oiled in sunlight
is water, the source
to which they flow.

As a herder, you may run about
restlessly, trying to dam
the course of the flood with a pebble,
poking an ineffectual stick
against brute hide;
or squat down, watching the great moon
set luminary sails
above the forest of muzzles,
hatched and blazoned emblems of thirst,
and feel the buck
in the embrace of the young leopard
who has forgotten the etiquette of the pool,
listen to the chill,
when the velvet lips stop nuzzling;
or trudge off, crook lowered,
looking for a tamer flock to bell,
the imprint of the day's sun
an unhealed sore on the back.

Beewoman

Bulging and pullulating
with fruiting bodies of bees,
the beewoman's hat hums
talkatively. Brimming
with brown, honey-striped
creatures, dripping down
from the rim as slow
as mead, it is less a hat
than a temporary hive;
home to a tribe in transit.

How does she hear her thoughts?
Perhaps her bees
embody them,
active hieroglyphs
charging the white page
of her veil with messages.

As lichen grows into rock
creating soil, so woman
and bees exchange wisdom,
distil into mutual honeycombs
news of a golden citadel
where wealth is stored
against the long attrition
of a sleeping sun.

The beewoman, heavy and awkward
as a ship, dipping with cargo,
is midwife to our fields.
Barren grasses, empty stores
wait the shimmering
tongues of bees.

Rustle and rattle

There are sounds we cannot hear:
the light patter of crab's claws
on the ocean floor; friction
of tiny joints as insects mate;
the gelid suck of soil in the worm's
wake, and planetary dust settling
millenia away. We are deaf
to the pleasant rustle of blood, tidally
lapping through flesh and bone -
though the heart, sluice-gate tuned
to the job of quelling
turbulent floods, amplifies its sound,
gives out resonant drub and knock,
loud as wavesmack in storm.

The ear's attentive fine-haired drum
vibrates to coarse grained noise
and puckers to sound so deep
it's heard as silence.
We know the note before it strikes;
snake's rattle, sift of dust,
the rustle in death's throat.

October gales

Mad as a young carthorse,
wind thunders across flat fields,
neighing and trumpeting,
pushing fences flat,
rolling on elastic withies
so they spring up, electrified.

The whole landscape
seethes like a satellite picture;
roiling craters in grass
boil over, a rush of silver lava
flooding to the field's brim.

To be outside,
where leaves are golden bullets,
is to know yourself porous;
brittle and careful
as an eggshell.

But inside, the house leaks
like a bird's nest, bright chinks
joining up as the tiles fly off.
And yesterday I watched a bend
in the nearby river,
its swollen sinews rippling
like great cables,
its brown elastic skin swelling
out of its sleeve.
At the heel of October,
when the horse of the gales
may run mad,
all our structures tumbling
like straw filled divots
from its streaming fetlocks,
it is better to know you
may be blown out and go
like a spark,
not hoard in sullen
charcoal dark a pinch of flame.

Night driving

The moon like a good child
lays its round cheek
on a pillow of cloud.
Black watered silk
the road unreels.

Spooled out forever
we roll into spilled sky,
clear water stained
by inky trees; this steel box
a bearing on the world's rim,
a toy hoop skimming
in a trance of light.
Silence is answered
by the hush of tyres.
I am small
in this reflection
of a sleeping sun;
skin coracle on
a luminous sea.

Split like a melon
the round horizon
falls apart; a cone
of headlights grows
from the hill.
Motorway lights,
orange lichens,
spring up,
cultured across the plate of dark.

Now I am driven,
gripping the wheel,
strapped in, captain
of our direction.

The moon's innocent apple
is half eaten;
I sense its dark cheek
hidden behind the light.

Persona

Every evening I put her
in the wardrobe.
She is too tall
to hang from the rail
so I clothespeg
her fashionably cut hair
to a cup hook.
Her braced shoulders
keep suits severely smart.
Empty eyeholes stare
as I step,
peeled as a willow stick,
white in the dusk of the room.

Now I can sip silence,
hear the bat-winged
passing of seconds,
feast on the green garden
till it turns to rustling
cut-out black.
Once, alerted by a particular
coolness, I looked in the mirror,
saw tiger lilies
sprung from my scalp.

Hard to wake
to the thumping
trochees and dactyls of the day;
to struggle into brittle skin,
moulding and patting,
easing on fingers and toes,
getting a good fit
under the arms.

Suppose I could pour myself in
wetly as an elver,
as a snake pours itself out
of its split skin in spring;
suppose I could walk
on the water of my night spirit,
strong as a salmon
in the day's upstream flow?

Open, visible and soft
like glow-worm tracks,
the day's scars would gleam
in the dusk.

Metamorphosis

Night burns on my pillow
like the open eye of sleep.

No escape. She watches;
her owl-eye slit, unblinking.

To go in through that narrow
black door, drawn utterly

to blood velvet dark,
beyond raw, gritty wakefulness

and find a dream on the far side
of sleep, or blackness past knowing,

needs my mouse under the night's
stare to turn hawk and find wings.

Scenes from a disorderly life

Washbasin birdlimed,
dessicated sponge,
dust on the mirror.

Why is the dirty clothes basket
full of dead skins?
Whose are those footprints
in talcum drifted
on the bathroom floor,
like Friday's feet
on the silent beach?

Inside my head
are rows of intransigent
hospital beds, their chill
sharp as a knife,
their symmetry flawless;
and books, pages
glued together,
spines ranged
against the shelf's edge,
their function to fill space.

Inside, a paralysis of order.
Outside, entropy drifts down,
insanitary, anarchic,
smelling of dirty washing
and drains, hinting
of secretions which only
lubricate the living.

On the hall floor
a bruised petal
speaks of life and death
in one red syllable.

For heart

Head's there,
gut's there,
where's heart?

Withered prune
written up
by poets,

excuse for
inflicting
damage

between lovers
and friends;
for kicking cats.

Not mislaid,
simply never
sought,

heart, drying out
like a mummified
mouse,

needs shock
treatment;
needs to jump

to know itself
alive; then
massage

by warm hands.
There you go
Heart,

have your eyes,
ears, nose and
guts back;

here's your head;
intelligent
Heart.

Adoption

Bundle the orphaned lamb
in borrowed wool,
in the fresh warm skin
of one newly dead.
Restless, the ewe
smells her own blood
on a soft fleece
and lets down
the consolation
of her milk
to the small hard mouth
of a made-over lamb,
always printed for its mother
with another's feel and smell.

Sheep absorb puzzlement
like rain on sweet turf,
though their voices
when the lambs go
lace the spring sun
from a fog of separation.

Do you see me now
in my skin, in my own skin,
printed with relics
of a child never yours?

I will wear your echoes
for company, a sonar
in the foggy fields of death,
though they come back
sounding of my voice.

I will lay the skin
of my cheek against yours.

Down the pan

On the infinite, shining
plains of Southend, a small
blip of movement. Freddie
the crab domesticates
that ringing salt space,
where Mum and Dad
fearlessly populate the sands.

Their legs are robustly planted,
my mother's round calves
whipped by her skirt,
my father'spolished toe caps
smudged with silt, his
trouser-legs banging
like flags, his trilby
clapped on square
to the wind.

They are going to ask me
impossible things; to build
a perfect sandcastle, to paddle
by myself.

Quick, into my red tin
bucket goes Freddie
and a hank of rubbery seaweed,
a brackish dash of puddle,
a small scuttling immolation
on the altar of family peace;
we all look at Freddie,
not at me.

Two days later, humped
on his dish in the bath,
his shell is dry, like
an egg from the saucepan,
his legs, no longer
jokey, witching wires,
are dangles of limp string.

My mother pronounces, "time
he went back to the sea."
I want to believe
in her tender, freckled hand
as she scoops him down the pan.

Gone

Is anything ever gone
or does it just bound
like a skimmed pebble
leaping over the sea's rim,
round and miraculously back?

I know when I hear gorse pop;
that dry, flat sound,
and see its yellow,
shrill on a dull day,
that goldfinches,
agile as crotchets,
will always burst out
from the bushes of childhood
where I collect seed,
foraging with my father,
between road and reservoir.

Always; not so resonant as gone;
that round, portentious
J. Arthur-Rank sound.
Will I always fritter
the dock's dry, brown heads
into my paper bag;
my mother flickering
like summer lightning,
cooking Sunday dinner
a mile away?

Home to Itma,
a smell of roast meat;
the dark brown bakelite
wireless crackling –
it tasted of bitter tobacco –
my strained antennae swivelling.

Always there,
packed in flavour and smell,
cabbage and Bisto;
red faces, raised voices,
stored in sharp
salt and vinegar bytes;
Smith's crisps;
tongue prickling lemonade;
a warm beer fug;
the opened door of a pub.

Always there, always gone,
like the closed door,
hushed on inexorable hinges;
then open in a magnesium flash.

I remember, always opening
on the strong hinge of gone.

Thyrotoxicosis

Under her size eighteen
I'd always suspected a witch.
Sure enough, she melted down.

Had I really done it?
My mother burned like a stick.
She blamed me. Her hands
clattered the pots
like chattering teeth.
Bolting around the kitchen
her eyes panicked,
hunting down why.

I'd always known
she didn't smell right;
they'd stolen me.

When I saw her, in perfect sheets,
quiet as a whisper, her deer's eyes
skittering mildly on white walls,
a white bandage on her throat,
I choked. My shaken flesh
leaned towards hers.
She tried to smile. I cried.
Ostermilk was thicker than blood.

Shrine of Our Lady of Dolour

Only the terrible goddess
is enshrined here,
loud with tinsel.
The hot breath
of a thousand candles,
greedy flames
from disappointed hearts,
licks the globe
she stands upon.

Incense masks the smell of blood;
seven and razor sharp,
the blades within her heart
are hidden
and honed for use.

Yet I would risk
the keen stripping
of flesh from bone
to see that other face
she shows her child.

My Father, counting sheep

He has been awake
for long enough, counting.
His life is thick, painful
seconds, squeezed from the glass.

Stretching his eyes behind
the sharp sun's lance
he waits
for the terrible medicine of dark.

He has his mother's eyes.
Often she rapped his head
with bony knuckles,
her fierce hazel glint
searching out sin like truffles.

She never cured him of looking;
silk in the rag bag,
silver in clouds.

Now, his rib cage winnowed
with scorching breath,
his big glove puppet hands
tell their own story
to the sheets.

Somewhere in the dry
fields of his brain
he is driving his last
ragged thoughts relentlessly,
over and over,
past the same gate,
counting to keep awake.

What gives him quiet?
Not me with my bolus
of love and drugs.
My mother, her voice
shrill with familiar strain,
whispers angrily tender,
"let GO!" He sighs.
His flocks line up soberly.
All the mild sheep
are folded through his eyes.

Katherine of Aragon buried briefly
in Peterborough Cathedral
and said, on the notice board, to have died of
cancer of the heart

Katherine died of cancer of the heart.
Terrifying. Apposite. Do we invite
the maggot best matched to our own dis-ease?
I think of her heart;
that bright apple, its firm flesh gnawed,
collapsed and rotten
as she strove to pack in
to the black hole at its core
all the faggots of righteous anger
that should have lit a gaudy bonfire
under the King.
His distemper grew outwards –
an opulent discharge
of pus and sloughed skin
falling like dandruff
on the nerves of courtiers,
subjects and wives.
We women and christians
are taught to forgive,
to consume our own smoke –
and other people's.
We die of cancerous forgiveness
like Katherine,
with that dark imploded star
at her centre; haven't learned
to burn off compromise, shabbiness,
collusion; to vent noxious gases;
to live with a hearth swept and bare.

For body bereaved

Sitting, backside dough-heavy
feet sprawled like left over boots,
abandoned body
composts sweat, snot, tears;
goes on in a lumpen
heap of fertile chemistry,
refuses to disappear
under the harrow.

I like your coarse
insistence on being here.
You won't join mind,
that gull, that winged ferret,
snapping up trifles
of consolation.

Perhaps our common
element is water.
Lifted off, like a heavy
anchor, lightly touching
bottom mud, pearled
with clean bubbles,
you could bend
and spring upright,
revolving slowly; released
from gravity in a spring tide.

Sometimes I long for dry land

Bag of blood,
twisted up with
red and blue knitting.
Heart, dumb fish,
sieving through its gills
deep indigo tides, red rapids.
Nothing separate
like leaves.

Even my bones
slip sideways,
red-washed, wet.
Not like the light
dry-point scatter
of bone from the
ocean-renouncing dead.

And my brain's
pea-princess refusal
not to be rock
is fretted by
surf and sea-weed.

I sway in my own tides,
that brassy paradox
bell in my throat
needing the opposition
of water to ring.

A small member

The tongue is a wicked implement.
Naturally wedge shaped, it functions
effectively as a pile driver,
scooping out the common ground
between lovers, friends and nations.

Silver or brazen; purveying, persuasive;
or leaping black and bitter
from the squeezed throat of a felon,
it cannot be trusted to tell the truth
until purged.

Only after the tongue has learned
to carry to the palate the taste
of salt, of bread, of wine, of empty air;
and flexed its muscles
as an implement of love,
is it fit to make words.

Witnesses

All things are made of the same stuff –
if I see, why can't they?
Why doesn't the newspaper fold up,
angular with despair, like an origami
albatross, weeping ashes?
Why doesn't the earth
slough us off like gangrene?
Why doesn't the sea leap up
like the great wall of China
and cough out our rubbish?

They say that sub-atomic particles
have memory. How can they be
so stolid? Why not, trembling
with rage, dance to a new pattern –
melt us down?

Silent witnesses – things – absorb,
soak up, watch, apparently unchanged;
their blind molecular clocks
ticking unmoved.

But sometimes, at dead of night,
I have heard heavy furniture
cry like a frightened child;
or seen in daylight, stones
made catatonic with old pain.
And panic flares, mixed with hope
that somewhere, deep beneath
its passive skin, our world's not mocked.

A visit to the camp museum

Our party scrunches
up a gravel drive
glinting like doll's eyes;
pine trees march
to the edge of moleskin lawns.
Beneath the trees
humus grows slowly
in an acid waste
of too few insects
and no worms.

The camp itself, collected,
as if just wrung
from disinfectant
by the disciplined mops
of barely absent soldiers
sprawls, almost transparent,
empty of smells and cries,
staunched and mopped
by absorbent pines.

We cannot raise our voices.
The flicker of a thousand newsreels
is drowned in green;
the hearts first fish-like
leap towards memories
not ours, is gaffed
and swallowed in a net of silence.

Here is a room poised to live,
needing only the tick
of logs in the grate.
Roses shed fragrance
on the curtain's sail.
Near the black, dumb
telephone is a lamp
with yellowing skin shade.

Somebody still
dusts it every day.

Dragon's teeth
The rare bee orchid has a dormancy period
of up to seven years

It is Sunday in the local woods.
Naturalists scatter like ducklings,
searching the bushes. Here you can see
one hundred and thirty seven moths,
six kinds of sedge. Puffs of nature
make you sneeze; flosses of silk
on the rushes, milky clouds
bundling over the rose-bays,
brown bloomed grass plumes,
catches of fluff in the willow.

Here where unsuspected ribs
of bony concrete catch your feet,
soft underlay of moss
obscures the shredded black
of runways. Once the tarmac
lit by swivelling owl-eyed
searchlights pointed
fat bellied bombers home
across a harvest moon.

Now plump and blond,
the fields beyond the wood edge
lie tranced all week,
unmoved, and only lurch
at the heel of a crop spray plane.

Patched over bomb store,
sorrel starting through its mortar;
faded KEEP OFF signs;
a village near, of pocked
red brick; a cupola'd church,
its skewed, once elegant
windows of cloud filled glass

keeping in the chilly smell
of worship, for six old women,
one priest and a boy,
are all set down like toys
on humps and hollows
of long filled ditches
and forgotten walls.

Here a soldier, pensioned off
and out to grass
took down his legionary sword
and once a week
spat to polish up old times.

Rich and complex as root
matts, as rank and living,
our Sunday gravy,
News of the World,
botanizing, snoozing,
praying Sabbath occupations
infiltrate the past;
join us with ghosts.

We are bound by bricks
and fields to summer
in this place, distilled
through the sleepy
throat of a hen.

In the woods, merciful
Dark Age weeds butt
and break belligerent stones,
clot once deadly paths,
staunch airstrip wounds
with pads of fragrant moss.

Sunday naturalists
glazed from reciting

litanies in the sun
come at last
to the rare bee orchid.

The pendulous lower lip
nudged by a look-alike bee
spits seed to spring
from gravid earth
by magic in seven summers –
better than dragon's teeth.

Reflections

Fish in the sky
among mackerel shoals;
something is hidden
by rain and day.

A bent pin and patience
are all you need;
no smoke stacks, winches
engines, nets.

You cannot trawl;
attentions steady pulse
drowns the shy catch
in its wake.

Fading circles leave
a queasy ghost
of motion; slowly
rocking water.

Through half closed lids
wait for the flash;
open; fix the image;
the one that got away;

till, silver faded,
grain rubbed out,
an empty print
curls downstream.

Gertrude Jekyll's boots

Heavy as loam, clogged
instep and welt, Gertrude's
wrinkled cast-offs
stand toe to toe,
slow-worm laces falling
down steep slopes, tongues
lolling like hounds after
a long chase. The shape
of her bunions is moulded
in onion domes;
her old, thick ankles
once puffed out the sides
like self-important
cheeks. More than
a death mask they
are a cast of life;

her death is live with flowers.

Next of kin

She is late Christmas shopping,
forging through soft golden drizzle,
wet, raw streets, dizzy lights,
no time to waste, mind on her list;
Aunt, nephew, secretary, godchild:
tick, tick. Not knowing
the heart in her side
will lie down, desperate
as a tired animal.

Cracked ice of pain
slams her flat.

Cold, so cold; jelly smeared,
wired, taped. A sharp
breeze of oxygen. Needle bright
lights. "Who is your next
of kin?" Her mouth
is too wounded to speak,
her ruined heart stutters.
"You are, sister, in your
merciful dark blue: none
ever closer."

Yellow pepper, orange pepper

On a white table
in a sunny room
yellow pepper, orange pepper,
curved strongly as buttocks,
gleaming like flesh,
a vivid lick of lime green stalk
laid over the cleft.

Gravid with light they sit;
I feel their weight
small but fleshly firm
on the tense skin
of a white dish.

Happiness breaks out
so sharp and deep
my sudden tears
become a globe
holding one golden sun.

Making all kinds of music

She is making full-hearted
sweeps with her bow.
Mozart? Liszt? Her elbow
pushes back heavy air,
then arcs down,
freighted with sound.

Her body sways,
breasts circling hips.
She is making a round
space in the music.

Outside in the street
I see honeysuckle
open its lion mouth,
shoot out a curly red tongue,
lick the wet wind.

I can't hear the rough throated
rasp of her music, but I feel
it flow down my bones.
Thick window glass
is suddenly permeable
to cold, wild honeysuckle
and a shiver of notes.

Lot's wife

What happened to Lot's wife?
Running with pretended vigour
to a virtuous future
she didn't want,
she stole a glance
at the laid-back, loose mouthed
city of sin, and turned
into a pillar of rectitude.

She would be there today,
somewhat eroded by harsh winds
and aching for rain,
but cattle of the night came,
soft, big, blundering
moth-mouthed creatures,
and licked her away.

Bede's tomb in Durham Cathedral

His slab, heavy as dark water.
My hand makes a hot print.
I speak to him. Round as ears
the rows of dogtoothed arches
bite off silence. I see
clear as a fossil in his waterstone
a skull, its tender knobs
rubbed like yellow candle wax.
Netsuke small, he is swaddled
in his fine shawl of dust,
his bird's foot fingers bent.

Silence; a great glittering space
of sea between pillars.
People still kneel before him,
bundle of twigs and parchment.

In the open ear of his grave
history goes on whispering
its fragments, nearer the ground
than truth: blood and stories.

Angel hair

Stiff as a cartwheel
hospital lawns
hubbed, one flaming
central multicelled
eye of flowers.

She stands upstairs
in a slim window
waiting. The mad
eye of the blazing
bee watches her;
its green velvet
coat seductive;
she hears its purr
rumbling; feels
the tide of honey
lap round its heart.

In the dim ward
stripped beds stand
empty as insect bones.

Nurse rattles
in the far-off sluice.

Blinking its white
eye the tv tics.

She stands, feral as a flower,
wrapped in her quiet wildness;
blue at her wrist and throat,
a stain of pigment.

Our DNA is simple
as a child's popper
beads, related
in blessed ordinariness
to the gruff blood
of elephants and whales;
but hers has a thread
of angel hair wound in;
she sees the live composite
beast below the world's
drab coat; here its eye
blazes out; there its
creaturely muscles move;
she catches a snatch
of its colour; smells
its breath; hears its voices,
intimate as gold and strange
as the wild luminary hair of heaven.

Stone ground

Can't catch me.
Thin as a bird
I scuttle on the floor
of your hopes.
Leaf in the wind.

> Drink your milk.
> Eat up.
> Clean your plate.
> Pipes, organs,
> gristle, fat,
> all that oozes,
> smells of death
> MAKES YOU STRONG
> . . . . . think of all the
> other little girls
> soldiers and sailors
> YOU'LL SIT THERE
> TILL YOU DO

I will grow
subtle as wind
in water; transitory
as a lean fox;
transparent as ice;
weightless as smoke.

My face will be
like evening,
a strip of fading gilt.

But if I grow up
poetry will be
the plain white
enamel of the fridge door.

Midnight
icicles crackle
like popsicles
cold sausages
grease blebs
chilled lips
Bunter custard
pies shivering
yesterday's barbequed
ribs stuck
to a white plate.

WHY DON'T YOU
join Weightwatchers
stop drinking
buy a good girdle
wax your legs
look after yourself
. . . . . be like
the others?

Why don't I
put a kind finger
on her mirrored lips?
say "look, we can
stop this now, this
nagging echo".

Only the strong
stone ground
bread of separation
fills the void of parting.
Let's eat!

A lecture on the conservation of stone

We see foreign trees
weeping January on sepia slides.
The monument is dark
and shaggy at bottom right.
Top left, white sky.
Fly specks stand in for birds.

His voice, speaking
of "the King's castle, maded
in stone, important for Poland",
is thin as worn reed thatch;
collapses as he wanders from the mike.

Lime water...baryta..pouring...
he is chest deep in courses
we've forgotten....recrystallisation?

Slow, dazzling growth
of native substance;
familiar crystal habit transformed.

We are used to thrusting in
tested foreign material.
He is like a unicorn.

His shy smile flashes;
his thin thread of voice
catches the light.

Faces opening

Suddenly all those faces
sculpted in blue shadow
on snow, open. Frozen
water sublimes, gutters
chuckle, tears run freely.

We're all in it together,
a pool where fish signal
comma or elipsis, single
and silver, running light
under the skin of water.

My fingers, ten small
drums beat painfully,
returning blood skintight.

I am like Kay, the splinter
has melted from my heart.
Whose tears dissolved it?

Yes: all I can find to say:
this is how we knew it would be;
but the sight of all our faces
opening like clouds, or mouths
lifted, hungry for rain, clears
the enigma from the dream;

                         spells YES.